Sam the Man & the Chicken Plan

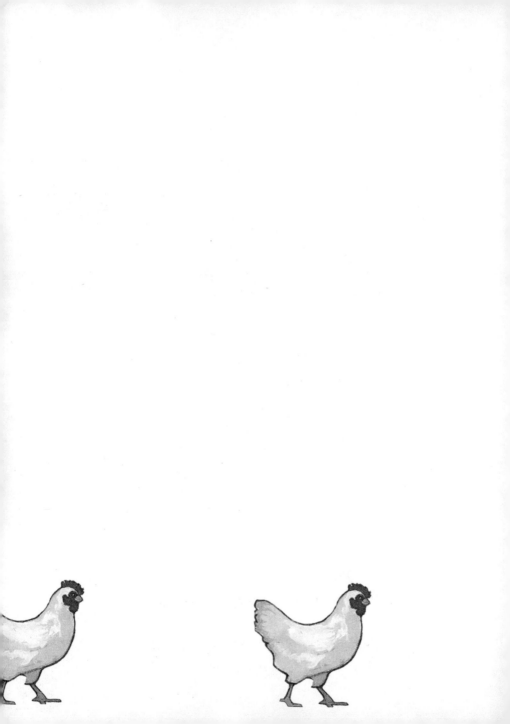

SAM THE MAN

& the Chicken Plan

FRANCES O'ROARK DOWELL

illustrated by **Amy June Bates**

A Caitlyn Dlouhy Book

Atheneum Books for Young Readers

atheneum New York London Toronto Sydney New Delhi

atheneum

ATHENEUM BOOKS FOR YOUNG READERS
An imprint of Simon & Schuster Children's Publishing Division
1230 Avenue of the Americas, New York, New York 10020
ATHENEUM BOOKS FOR YOUNG READERS is a registered trademark of Simon & Schuster, Inc.
Atheneum logo is a trademark of Simon & Schuster, Inc.
For information about special discounts for bulk purchases, please contact Simon & Schuster Special Sales at 1-866-506-1949 or business@simonandschuster.com.
The Simon & Schuster Speakers Bureau can bring authors to your live event. For more information or to book an event, contact the Simon & Schuster Speakers Bureau at 1-866-248-3049 or visit our website at www.simonspeakers.com.
Also available in an Atheneum Books for Young Readers hardcover edition
Book design by Sonia Chaghatzbanian
The text for this book was set in New Century Schoolbook.
The illustrations for this book were rendered in pencil.
Manufactured in the United States of America
0117 MTN
First Atheneum Books for Young Readers paperback edition February 2017
10 9 8 7 6 5 4 3 2 1
The Library of Congress has cataloged the hardcover edition as follows:
Dowell, Frances O'Roark, author.
Sam the man and the chicken plan / Frances O'Roark Dowell. — First edition.
pages cm
ISBN 978-1-4814-4066-0 (hc)
ISBN 978-1-4814-4067-7 (pbk)
ISBN 978-1-4814-4068-4 (eBook)
1. Chickens—Juvenile fiction. 2. Money-making projects for children—Juvenile fiction. 3. Families—Juvenile fiction. [1. Chickens—Fiction. 2. Moneymaking projects—Fiction. 3. Family life—Fiction.] I. Title.
PZ7.D75455Sam 2016
813.6—dc23
[Fic]
2015007119

For my dear friend and superstar librarian
Michelle Rosen
—F. O. D.

For Emily and her chickens
—A. J. B.

CHAPTER 1

A Job for Sam

Sam Graham wanted a job.

Everyone else in his family had a job. His dad did something with computers, and his mom did something with clients, and his sister, Annabelle, who was twelve, mowed lawns.

"Twenty bucks a pop," Annabelle said when she came home from a job, sweaty and flecked with little bits of grass. "Hard to beat."

"What can I do for twenty bucks a pop?" Sam asked his mom.

"There aren't many jobs for seven-year-olds," his mom said. "I'll give you a dollar to clean your room."

Sam didn't want a job that only paid one buck a pop.

Besides, his room didn't need cleaning.

When Mrs. Kerner stopped by to see if Annabelle would take care of her chickens while she was away, Annabelle said she couldn't do it.

"I have three lawns to mow this weekend," she told Mrs. Kerner. "Hate to say it, but there's no time for chickens."

Sam raced over to Mrs. Kerner. He waved his arms in the air. "I'll take care of your chickens!"

"You're only seven," Mrs. Kerner said.

"Seven-year-olds don't know the first thing about chickens."

"I know they lay eggs," Sam said, holding up one finger.

"I know they like to be around other chickens," he added, holding up a second finger.

He tried to think of one more thing he had learned on the second-grade field trip to the farm.

Aha! He held up a third finger. "I know their poop is good for the garden."

"Don't say 'poop,'" said Mrs. Kerner.

"I like the way it sounds," said Sam.

"Still," said Mrs. Kerner. "Still and all."

She looked at Sam for a long time. "You know a lot about chickens. But you're awfully small."

"I'm bigger than a raccoon," said Sam.

"I despise raccoons," said Mrs. Kerner.

"Me too," said Sam.

"Okay, then," said Mrs. Kerner. "I think we can work together."

CHAPTER 2

Don't Forget the Chickens

Sam's chicken job started on Friday afternoon. Friday morning, Sam ate eggs for breakfast, to get ready.

"Don't forget the chickens, Sam the Man!" his dad called on his way out of the house.

"I won't," said Sam.

"Don't forget the chickens, Sam," his mom said not two minutes later, putting papers in her briefcase.

Sam huffed and puffed. "I said I *won't*."

"How much are you getting paid?" is what Annabelle said.

Sam didn't know. He had forgotten to ask.

"Twenty bucks a pop," he decided.

Friday afternoon Sam went to work.

The chickens lived in a coop in Mrs. Kerner's backyard, which was four backyards down from Sam's. Mrs. Kerner had only had her chickens for three weeks, so Sam didn't know them very well.

When the chickens saw Sam, they squawked. They strutted. They puffed out their chests.

Sam scooped grain into the chickens' feeder, just the way Mrs. Kerner had shown him. He picked out a leaf from their water bowl. When he was done, he carefully latched the door to the coop so that no raccoons could get in.

On Saturday morning Sam filled the feeder and added water to the bowl. He collected the chickens' eggs and had an omelet for breakfast.

After lunch Sam's friend Gavin came over, and they built a fort out of branches and rocks in the backyard.

Then they filled up thirty-six balloons with water and had a water balloon fight.

Then Sam used his mom's blow-dryer to dry Gavin off before his dad picked him up.

"Don't forget the chickens," Sam's mom said as they waved good-bye to Gavin and his dad.

"I won't," said Sam.

7

He put on some dry socks.

"Don't forget the chickens," his dad said as he passed Sam in the hallway.

"I said I *won't*," Sam said.

When Sam got to Mrs. Kerner's yard, the chickens were making a racket. They squawked and clucked. Sam looked around. At the edge of the yard sat a fat raccoon.

"Go away!" Sam yelled.

The raccoon just sat there.

Sam double-checked the lock and then ran home. He got his sleeping bag, his tent, and a box of raisins.

He told his mom he was spending the night with the chickens.

"I don't think so," said his mom.

"Not a good plan, Sam the Man," said his dad.

That night Sam couldn't sleep.

He could not forget the chickens.

Maybe he should call the police. Maybe they could arrest the raccoon.

He got up. He stood outside his parents' bedroom.

"I can't forget the chickens!" he yelled.

CHAPTER 3

Twenty Bucks a Pop

Annabelle opened her door.

"It's two a.m.," she said.

"What if the raccoon eats the chickens?" Sam asked.

"That would be bad," Annabelle said. "I'll get the flashlight."

When they got to Mrs. Kerner's yard, the chickens were fine. The raccoon was nowhere to be seen.

"I think we should stay," Sam said.

"Okay," Annabelle said. "Go grab the lawn chairs from Mrs. Kerner's deck."

"It's peaceful here," she said after they sat down.

"It won't be when the chickens wake up," Sam said.

But the chickens didn't wake them up. Mrs. Kerner did.

"I'm home early," she said. "How much do I owe you?"

"We stayed here all night," Sam said. "We protected the chickens against a raccoon."

"What will that run me?" asked Mrs. Kerner.

"Twenty bucks a pop," Sam said.

"I'll give you ten," said Mrs. Kerner.

"I'd rather have twenty," said Sam.

"I suppose," said Mrs. Kerner. "You did stay up all night."

She gave him a crisp, green-gray twenty-dollar bill.

Sam sniffed it. It smelled good.

Sam and Annabelle walked home. Sam got back into bed. He slept for a long time.

There was a knock on the door.

"Don't forget the chickens!" his mom said.

Sam rolled over.

He would never forget the chickens.

CHAPTER 4

Money to Burn

Sam was ready to spend his twenty dollars. But twenty dollars was too much and not enough.

Twenty dollars was too much to spend on candy, even if it was fun to think about how much candy twenty dollars would buy.

Twenty dollars was not enough money for a Marsville Mudcats' shirt like the one Sam's favorite player, Evan Faruk, wore.

Twenty dollars was too much for a Marsville Mudcats' keychain.

Besides, Sam didn't have any keys.

If he had a car, he would have a key, but twenty dollars was not enough for a car. Not even a beat-up jalopy like his aunt Sarah drove.

"You don't have to spend it all at once," Sam's mom said. "You could spread it out."

Sam didn't like spreading out money. The last time he spread out money, he'd ended up with:

1. a koala bear bookmark from the science museum,
2. eight gumball machine tattoos,
3. a beef jerky stick from the checkout line at the grocery store.

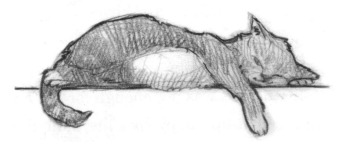

Spreading out money was a good way to get a whole bunch of nothing.

Sam went next door to see his neighbor Judy. Judy was a semi-old person who took care of her very old dad, Mr. Stockfish, and Mr. Stockfish's five cats.

"I'll tell you what your problem is," Judy told Sam when he'd asked her how he should spend his twenty dollars. She was folding laundry in the living room while she and Mr. Stockfish watched the all-day news channel.

"What's my problem?" Sam asked.

"The best things in life are free," Judy

said. "True happiness doesn't cost a dime, much less twenty dollars."

Mr. Stockfish snorted. He was sitting in his puffy chair with a knob he could twist to make it go higher or lower. "Cable TV isn't free," he said.

"It is if your mom and dad pay for it," Sam said.

Mr. Stockfish waved his hand like Sam's words were flies buzzing around his head.

That was his way of saying he was done talking.

"Let me show you something," Judy said to Sam. She picked up a book from the coffee table and pulled a red bookmark from its pages. Stepping closer, Sam realized Judy was showing him a red feather.

"This didn't cost anything," Judy said. "But it makes me happy every time I look at it."

She handed the feather to Sam. "You can have it. Maybe it will bring you good luck. Maybe it will help you figure out the best way to spend twenty dollars."

Sam took the feather and thanked Judy. Then he went home. He climbed the stairs to his room and sat on his bed. He looked at the feather. He stared at it without blinking for ten seconds, and then he shut his eyes tight.

He still didn't know how to spend his twenty dollars.

Annabelle poked her head into his room.

"It's a mess in here," she said, pointing to his floor, which was covered with socks and tiny plastic building bricks and Popsicle sticks he was collecting to build a race car with.

"I like it messy," Sam told her.

Annabelle nodded. "Me too. Messy is best. Too bad Mom doesn't think so."

"Where'd you get that shirt?" Sam asked.

Annabelle's shirt was five times too big for her and had pictures of red and green parrots all over it.

"It's Dad's. Mom was trying to throw it away, but I rescued it."

"I didn't know Dad liked parrots so much," Sam said.

"I think he only likes them on shirts," Annabelle said. "So, what's that?"

Sam held up his feather. "Judy gave it to me. For good luck."

"It looks like a lucky feather," Annabelle said. "In fact, it could be a magic feather."

Sam rolled his eyes. "There's no such thing as magic feathers."

Annabelle shrugged. "Maybe not. But definitely lucky feathers. In fact, I've got just the thing for your lucky feather."

"What?" Sam asked.

"Follow me," Annabelle said.

They walked across the hall to Annabelle's bedroom. "You need a special box to keep your lucky feather in," Annabelle said. She opened her closet door and pointed to a stack of shoe boxes.

"I have lots of shoe boxes, but I'm using them to stash my lawn-mowing money in," Annabelle said. "I'm saving up for a goat."

"What do you need a goat for?" Sam asked.

"Goats eat grass. When I get my goat, I'm going to rent it out to our neighbors who think lawn mowers are too noisy."

Sam liked that idea. Maybe he could be

the person who held on to the goat's rope while it ate.

"Now, I do have a very special box," she said. "But it's much too special to give away."

"Could I borrow it?" Sam asked. The more he thought about it, the more he wanted a box for his feather.

Besides, he really liked boxes.

"You could buy it," Annabelle said.

She pulled down a wooden box from the closet shelf. It was the size of two large tissue boxes taped together.

"How much?" Sam asked.

"Twenty bucks," she said.

Sam looked at the box closely. The lid was attached with two hinges and had a clasp so you could shut it tightly.

Sam liked lids with clasps.

"I'll take it," he said.

He ran back to his room and got his crisp, good-smelling, green-gray twenty-dollar bill from under his pillow.

It had gotten a little wrinkled since the last time he'd seen it.

He would miss it.

CHAPTER 5

The Bluebird of Happiness

Sam took his box over to Mrs. Kerner's. The chickens clucked and squawked when they saw him.

"I'm starting a feather collection," he told Mrs. Kerner when she came to the back door. "I thought some chicken feathers might be nice, if that's okay."

"You can have whatever feathers you find on the ground," Mrs. Kerner said. "And

I have a special feather I will add to your collection."

A few minutes later Mrs. Kerner came out of her house carrying a small, blue feather.

"It's not a chicken feather," she said. "But it's special all the same. It is a feather from the bluebird of happiness."

"Is there only one?" Sam asked.

"There are many blue feathers, but only one bluebird of happiness."

Sam took the feather and said thank you.

Then he carefully put the blue feather in the box next to his red feather and closed the clasp.

"Only feathers you find on the ground!" Mrs. Kerner reminded Sam as he started looking around the coop. "No plucking!"

"I would never pluck," Sam said, offended that Mrs. Kerner thought he might.

Unfortunately, the only feathers on the ground that day were the little downy feathers that stuck to his fingers when he tried to pick them up. He decided not to collect annoying feathers.

"I'll come back tomorrow," he told Mrs. Kerner. "Maybe some of the chickens will shed overnight."

"Chickens don't shed; they molt," Mrs. Kerner told him. "But it's almost the molting time of the year. You should come back every day, just in case."

If Sam didn't know better, he might think Mrs. Kerner liked having him around. He guessed he liked being around. Mrs. Kerner seemed mean when you first met her, but after a while she turned out to be sort of nice. Her niceness was like a secret that only a few people knew about.

Sam carried the box home, being careful to walk slowly and not trip over any cracks in the sidewalk.

That night at dinner Sam made an announcement. "I have a feather from the bluebird of happiness."

"I'd rather have a pie from the blueberry of happiness," Annabelle said. She grinned at Sam, so he could see the macaroni and cheese stuck in her braces.

"There is no blueberry of happiness," Sam told her.

"I wonder if there's a blue moon of happiness," his mom said.

"Or a blue plate special of happiness," his dad said.

Sam ate a bite of mac and cheese, and then he took another bite. It might be a few minutes before his parents stopped being silly.

"I wonder if it would be okay to take my feather collection to school," he said when everyone quieted down. "Do you think someone would steal it?"

"You could ask Mr. Pell to keep it in his desk drawer," Annabelle said. "The one with the lock on it."

Sam stared at his sister. "How do you know about the drawer with the lock on it? You were never in Mr. Pell's class."

"All teachers have at least one drawer that locks," Annabelle explained. "It keeps people from stealing their lunch bags."

Sam had seen what Mr. Pell brought for lunch. Usually, he had a stinky tuna fish sandwich, an apple with brown spots, and kale chips.

Sam didn't think Mr. Pell needed to worry about anyone stealing his lunch bag.

Still, he was glad Annabelle had reminded him about the desk drawer that locked. Sam was pretty sure it was big enough for his box.

After dinner Sam went to his room. On his way up the stairs, he started thinking about people who might steal his feather collection.

Number one on his list was Emily Early. Emily was crazy about birds. On weekends her family went to parks and looked at birds through their binoculars. Once, for show-and-tell, Emily brought in a notebook where she'd written the name of every kind of bird she'd ever seen.

The list was sixty-eight birds long.

Boy, oh boy, would Emily Early like to get her hands on a feather from the bluebird of happiness!

Connor Ross might also try to steal Sam's collection.

That was because Connor Ross was a creep.

Sam knocked on Annabelle's door. "Maybe it's too risky to take my feathers to school," he said when she came to the doorway.

Annabelle shrugged. "Life is full of risks, Sam the Man. To share or not to share? That's the question. But my question is, why have something special if you can't show it to other people?"

"That's a good point," Sam said.

"All my points are good points," Annabelle said. "Any other questions?"

That was the only question Sam had, so he went to his room.

The box with Sam's feathers was sitting on his desk. He had left the lid open, so his feathers could breathe.

He'd also left his window open, so his feathers could feel the nice, evening breeze.

Sam walked over to the box. He looked inside.

The box was empty.

Someone had stolen his feathers!

He couldn't believe it. A robber must have climbed through his open window and taken it!

"Come back with my feathers!" he yelled out the window.

But nobody yelled back.

Sam's collection was gone.

CHAPTER 6

The Case of the Missing Feathers

Everyone rushed into Sam's room.

"What happened, Sam?" asked his dad.

"Are you okay?" asked his mom.

"I'm fine," Sam said. "But my feathers are missing! A robber must have gotten them!"

Annabelle walked over to Sam's open window. "Or else they flew away."

"Feathers can't fly by themselves," Sam said.

"They can if the wind helps them," Annabelle said.

Sam thought about this. It made sense. The feathers had probably flown away on a nice breeze.

Sam peered out the window into the dark backyard. He could see branches moving from side to side. He leaned his head against the window frame, feeling tired and sort of sad. He would never find his feathers tonight.

"I'll get up first thing in the morning and look for them," he said.

"Don't get your hopes up too high, Sam the Man," said his dad. "They may have flown out of town by then. It's pretty windy out there."

His dad was right. The next morning Sam couldn't find his feathers anywhere.

"At least now you don't have to worry about your collection getting stolen," Annabelle said as they walked to the bus stop.

Not a helpful comment, Sam thought.

Sam had looked forward to carrying his box up the steps to the bus. He had looked forward to Miss Louise, the bus driver, making guess after guess about what was inside. He had looked forward to letting Gavin take a peek, but nobody else.

Instead, when Sam got on the bus, he said, "Hi, Miss Louise," and Miss Loiuse said, "Hello, Sam the Man," and that was it.

Gavin had saved him a seat. "Guess what I brought for show-and-tell?" he asked Sam.

"Wookie the Sock Monkey?" Sam guessed.

"How did you know?" Gavin sounded disappointed that Sam had guessed correctly.

"You always bring Wookie the Sock Monkey for show-and-tell."

Gavin nodded. "I like a routine."

"I lost what I was going to bring," Sam said. "So, I guess I don't have anything."

He hoped Gavin would ask him what he'd lost, but Gavin didn't. Instead, Gavin said, "I have an eraser you could show. I drew purple and green stripes on it with markers. Want it?"

Sam shook his head. "I'd rather not show anything, since I can't show this really special thing."

"A striped eraser is pretty special," Gavin said. "Most people would agree with me about that."

Sam gave up on waiting for Gavin to ask

him about the special thing he lost. "It was my feather collection, including a feather from the bluebird of happiness and a lucky red feather," Sam said. "That was my special thing."

"Wow!" Gavin's eyes got wide. "That sounds awesome! Where did you get the happiness feather?"

"Our neighbor Mrs. Kerner."

"How did she get it?" Gavin asked.

"I don't know," Sam said. "She didn't tell me."

"Do you think you could find another one?"

Sam thought about it. "Mrs. Kerner did say there was only one bluebird of happiness, but more than one feather."

"That settles it," said Gavin. "Meet me on the playground at recess."

"I always meet you on the playground at recess," Sam said.

"Yeah, but today we're going to do something different."

"We're not going to play soccer with Will and Rashid?"

"No," Gavin said. "We're going to find you another feather from the bluebird of happiness, so you'll have something to show at show-and-tell!"

"Where?" Sam asked.

"On the kickball field, of course," said Gavin.

Of course, Sam thought. Why hadn't he thought of that?

CHAPTER 7

Field of Feathers

Will and Rashid and Emily Early all wanted to help Sam and Gavin search the kickball field for feathers.

So did Emily's best friend, Imogene, a bossy girl who talked about horses as much as Emily talked about birds.

"Let's gallop!" Imogene yelled as they walked toward the kickball field. "Let's pretend we're a herd of golden palominos!"

Imogene and Emily galloped ahead. Sam

and Gavin and Will and Rashid all looked at one another and shook their heads.

"Why do girls like horses so much?" Rashid asked. "My sister is always begging my parents for a horse. She's got horse posters all over her room. But you know what? She's never ridden a horse in her whole life. She's never even touched one!"

"The twins make us watch *The Black Stallion* practically every night," Will said. "And I'm always stepping on their little horse guys."

Of all of Sam's friends, Will had the worst luck. His twin sisters, Maisy and Daisy, were in the fourth grade and famous for wearing matching outfits every single day. Also, Will's mom ran a ballet school.

Really, Sam thought, things could not be worse for Will.

"Found one!" Emily called from third base. "It was right here in the dirt."

The feather Emily found was a rusty brown. It was not a feather from the blue-bird of happiness.

Still, Sam took it from Emily and put it in the plastic bag Mr. Pell had given him for feather collecting. "Thanks," he said.

"De nada!" Emily said, and then she galloped over to centerfield. "I bet I'll find tons of feathers here!"

After a fifteen-minute search, the group had found a total of eight feathers.

Emily found two more rusty-brown feathers.

Rashid found two black-and-white feathers, and Will found two gray-and-white feathers.

Gavin and Sam found one at the same

time, a red feather that Emily thought probably came from a cardinal.

"If we were in South America, it might have come from a scarlet ibis," Emily said, holding out the red feather that looked like the one Judy had given Sam. "But since we live in North America, it probably didn't."

Walking back to the playground, Sam peered inside his bag of feathers. He guessed they looked nice, even if none of them was a feather from the bluebird of happiness.

"Maybe we'll find a blue feather tomorrow," Gavin said. "I don't think we should give up."

"Maybe," Sam said. "I guess I could show these feathers today for show-and-tell, if that's okay with everyone."

He tried to sound excited about it, but

Sam was starting to wonder if you could only be superexcited about feathers for twenty-four hours and after that your excitement was all used up.

"I'm showing my new book about horses at show-and-tell," Imogene said. "It's called *A Foal Is Born* by Danielle H. Paul. She's the leading horse expert in our state."

Sam turned to Emily. "Maybe you should do show-and-tell on the feathers. You're probably the leading bird expert in our state."

"That's okay, Sam," Emily said. "I brought in some pictures from my family's birding trip last weekend. You can tell about the feathers."

"After all, Sam, collecting the feathers was your idea!" Gavin said.

"I thought it was your idea," Sam said.

Gavin thought about this. "Oh, yeah, it was. Maybe I should talk about the feathers."

"You can't talk about the feathers!" Imogene said. "You have to talk about Wookie the Sock Monkey! If you didn't, then everyone would feel weird."

"That's true," Gavin said.

"I'll talk about the feathers, then," said Sam. "Just remember I'm not an expert."

Everyone agreed that Sam didn't have to be an expert on feathers to talk about them for show-and-tell.

Walking back into the school building, carrying his plastic bag with eight feathers, Sam realized that practically everyone he knew was an expert on something. Gavin was an expert on Wookie the Sock Monkey, Emily was an expert on birds, and Imogene was an expert on horses. Will was probably the world's greatest expert on bad luck and annoying twin sisters.

Sam wanted to be an expert on something, too.

But what?

CHAPTER 8

The Chicken Plan

I would like to get a chicken," Sam told his parents that night at dinner.

"To eat?" his mom asked. "We don't have any chicken, honey. Just spaghetti."

"Not to eat," Sam said. "To grow."

"I think you mean to raise," Annabelle said. "You *grow* carrots. You *raise* chickens."

"I would like to get a chicken to *raise*, so I can become a chicken expert," Sam said.

"Actually, I would like to get three chickens. Mrs. Kerner told me they don't like to live by themselves."

Sam's mom looked at Sam's dad like she was waiting for him to say something.

Sam's dad looked at Sam's mom like he was waiting for her to say something.

"I'll pay for it myself," Sam said.

"Where are you going to get the money?" Annabelle asked.

"I could help you mow lawns," Sam said. "Or you could pay me to hold the rope when you get your goat."

"You're getting a goat?" Sam's mom asked Annabelle.

"You are not getting a goat," Sam's dad said at the same time.

Annabelle looked at Sam. "Did you have to bring up the goat?"

47

"Sorry," Sam said. "Why don't we talk about chickens instead?"

"Good idea," said Annabelle.

"Where would you keep the chickens, Sam?" Sam's mom asked.

"In a coop," Sam said. "You have to put them in a coop every night and close it up tight, so the foxes and raccoons don't eat them."

"Not to mention the snakes," Annabelle added.

"Snakes?" Sam's mom asked. Her face got very pale. "Snakes eat chickens?"

"They eat their eggs," Annabelle said. "We saw a movie about it in science class."

No one said anything for a minute.

Then Sam's dad said, "Sam the Man, I have a plan. Why don't you ask Mrs. Kerner if you could add a chicken to her flock?"

"What do you mean?" Sam asked.

"You could get your own chicken, and it could live with Mrs. Kerner's chickens. Maybe you could do chores as a way to pay rent."

"That's a great idea!" Sam's mom said.

Sam thought about it. He thought it would be nicer if his chicken lived at his house, so he could see it whenever he wanted.

On the other hand he could become an even bigger chicken expert if he was around a lot of chickens at once. Mrs. Kerner had six chickens. If Sam got one chicken, that would be seven chickens.

Hanging out with seven chickens would make Sam a chicken expert in no time. There was only one problem he could think of.

"How will I know which eggs are mine?" he asked.

"Get the kind of chicken that lays green eggs," Annabelle said.

"There's a chicken that lays green eggs?"

"Pretty awesome, huh?"

Sam nodded. He imagined taking green eggs to school for show-and-tell.

Maybe he could take his chicken to show-and-tell!

He wondered if Miss Louise would let him bring his chicken on the school bus.

He was pretty sure she would.

CHAPTER 9

A Funny Name for a Chicken

Mrs. Kerner said Sam was welcome to add a chicken to her flock.

In return Sam would check the chickens' water every afternoon and clean the coop on Saturdays.

"That's it?" Sam asked her. "That's all I have to do to pay rent?"

Mrs. Kerner shrugged. "What can I say? Chickens are easy."

Now all Sam had to do was get his

chicken. He and his dad did some research and decided they would try to buy one from somebody nearby.

Sam's dad put a request in the classified section of the Marsville community's website. *Wanted,* he wrote. *One chicken, not too old. Must lay green eggs.*

The next day someone named Trisha Hardy e-mailed Sam's dad. "I have a chicken that lays blue eggs. In fact, I have five of them. I'm moving next month and need to find them new homes."

Sam's dad wrote back that they only wanted one chicken, and blue eggs were fine.

He and Trisha Hardy made plans for Sam and his dad to pick up the chicken.

"What are you going to name her?" Sam's dad asked on the ride over.

"How do we know it's a her?" Sam asked.

He didn't know if he wanted a girl chicken. Most of his friends were boys.

"All chickens that lay eggs are girls, Sam the Man," Sam's dad said. "They're called hens. Boy chickens are roosters."

Sam guessed he knew that already. He felt sort of dumb for forgetting.

"Could we get a rooster instead?" he asked.

"Nope, roosters are too noisy. In our neighborhood you can only have chickens. That's the rule. Besides, don't you want a chicken that lays eggs?"

Sam nodded. He'd like to see what a blue egg looked like. The only blue eggs he'd ever seen had been plastic.

Sam had thought that Trisha Hardy would live on a farm in the country. But she didn't. She lived in a subdivision called

Willow Oak, and her house looked a lot like Sam's house.

"Let me introduce you to Helga!" Trisha Hardy said when Sam and his dad got out of the car. "She's out back with the rest of the girls."

"You can change the name," Sam's dad whispered to him.

Sam was happy to hear that.

As soon as Sam saw Trisha Hardy's chicken coop, he wished they could have one too. It looked like a real house, with windows and a front door. If he had a chicken coop like that, maybe he could sleep in it during the summer.

"Here she is," Trisha said, carrying a chicken over to Sam and his dad. The chicken had reddish-brown feathers and red markings around her eyes and beak.

Trisha kissed the chicken on the head. "I'm going to miss her so much! Such a sweetie!"

Sam and his dad looked at each other. Sam's dad made a face.

Sam made a face back. Kissing chickens was gross.

"So, why don't you bring out the crate, and we'll get Helga settled," Trisha said.

Sam and his dad looked at each other again.

"We were supposed to bring a crate?" Sam's dad asked.

Trisha nodded.

"I think we might have forgot," Sam said.

"Hmm, let me think," Trish said. "I know! I have a box you could put her in. But someone will have to sit next to her in the car and keep her calm."

They put Helga's box in the backseat. Then Trisha gave Helga one last kiss, Sam's dad gave Trisha some money, and Trisha put Helga in the box.

Sam slid into the backseat next to Helga. He put on his seat belt.

"Do you think I should try to put a seat belt on Helga?" he asked his dad.

"Just hold on to the box, and I'll do my best not to crash the car," his dad said.

That sounded like a good plan to Sam.

"Stay calm," Sam told Helga as his dad backed the car down the driveway. "We only live five minutes away."

Helga squawked.

"How do you like the name 'Red'?" Sam asked her.

Helga squawked louder. She fluttered and flapped her wings. She started to hop.

"I don't think she's staying calm," Sam told his dad.

"Just keep her in the box," Sam's dad said.

Helga hopped a little higher. She squawked a little louder.

Sam held on to the box as tight as he could. "It's only a few more minutes, Helga," he said. "Why don't you take a nap until we get there?"

Helga took one last hop. She hopped so high she looked Sam straight in the eye.

It didn't look like she was going to fall asleep anytime soon.

"Squaawwk!" Helga squawked.

"Bawwk!" Helga bawked.

And then, with one flap of her wings, she was over the side of the box and headed for freedom.

CHAPTER 10

The Hopping Hen

Dad!" Sam yelled. "Helga escaped!"

"Keep calm, Sam the Man," his dad said. He pulled the car over to the side of the road. "Can you catch her?"

Sam reached down to grab Helga, who was on the floor in front of her box. She hopped to the left of his hands, and she hopped to the right. Then she hopped up into Sam's lap.

"I caught her," he told his dad.

"Well, hold on tight. I've got an idea."

Sam's dad got a blanket from the trunk of the car while Sam held on to Helga. Helga squawked, but she didn't seem to mind too much. Sam didn't mind either. Helga's feathers were soft. He could feel her little heart beating in her chest.

He sort of minded her claws, though. He wished they weren't so sharp.

"Let's put Helga back in her box and then put this blanket over the top," Sam's dad said. "Maybe if she can't see anything, she won't get so excited."

"I don't mind holding her," Sam said. "I think she likes being held."

Sam's dad looked doubtful, but he nodded. "Okay. We're almost home. Just don't let her hop up front."

Helga had stopped hopping. She sat on

Sam's lap for the rest of the ride and looked out the window. When they reached Mrs. Kerner's house, Sam told Helga, "This is where you're going to live. But I'll come visit you every day."

After he parked the car in Mrs. Kerner's driveway, Sam's dad turned around and said, "Don't forget, Sam—you promised you would pay for a chicken if we let you get one."

"I did?" Sam asked. He didn't remember that. He guessed it was fair, though.

"You did. Helga cost twenty dollars. You can pay me back a little every week."

Twenty bucks! Now, Sam wished he hadn't bought Annabelle's box.

Mrs. Kerner opened her front door and waved. "Did you get your chicken, Sam?"

"Her name is Helga," Sam said. He

popped out of the car. He was still holding Helga. "I was going to change it, but now she seems like a Helga to me."

"If it were up to me, I'd call her 'Janice,'" Mrs. Kerner said. "She looks like a Janice. But it's not up to me."

Sam, Sam's dad, and Mrs. Kerner walked to the backyard. "The other chickens might not be nice to Helga right away," Mrs. Kerner said. "At first, we're going to put her in a crate next to the coop. This lets the other birds get used to her."

"Won't she get lonely?" Sam asked.

"A little bit, maybe," Mrs. Kerner said. "But it's better than getting pecked."

Sam was happy to see that the crate was big. If Helga wanted to hop around, she would have plenty of room. The crate didn't have a bottom. When Sam put Helga inside, she began to peck at the dirt.

The other chickens looked very interested in Helga. They rushed to the edge of the coop nearest Helga's crate and clucked. The biggest chicken flapped her wings and shook her head. Sam thought she seemed mad.

He had never thought about chickens getting mad before. He didn't know that chickens had any emotions at all.

"Do you want to stay with Helga for a little while?" Sam's dad asked when he was ready to leave. Sam nodded.

"I want to see if she lays an egg," he said.

"She might not lay any eggs for a few days," Mrs. Kerner said after Sam's dad left. "She needs to settle in. But we'll get her a nest box to sit on, just in case."

"I have a box at home we could use," Sam said.

"It's probably not the right kind for laying eggs in," Mrs. Kerner said. "You can use one of mine."

Soon, Helga's crate was outfitted with a water bowl, a food trough, and a nesting box. Sam thought it looked like a comfortable setup. He pulled a lawn chair down

from the deck and settled in next to Helga. He wondered if she would lay an egg if he sang to her.

Probably not, he thought.

Besides, he would feel silly singing to a chicken.

"Take your time, Helga," he said, even though he was curious to see what a blue egg would look like.

He wondered how much money people would pay to see a blue egg?

He wondered how much money people would pay to *eat* a blue egg?

He leaned back in his chair and smiled.

Sam the Man had just come up with a how-to-pay-back-his-dad plan.

CHAPTER 11

A Change in Plans

A week had gone by, and Helga still hadn't laid an egg.

"Be patient," Mrs. Kerner told Sam. "A girl needs time to settle in."

Normally, Sam was a very patient person. But now he needed money to pay his dad, and twenty bucks was a lot of money.

On Friday night he knocked on Annabelle's door. "Would you like to buy back your box?" he asked. "I've only used it a couple of times."

"Sorry, Sam the Man, but I've got all the boxes I need," Annabelle said.

"Could I take one of your lawn-mowing jobs?"

Annabelle shook her head. "You're too small to mow the lawn. Maybe in three years."

"I need twenty bucks," Sam said. "And I need it before three years from now."

"That's a problem," Annabelle said. "You should ask Mrs. Kerner for a job. You know a lot about chickens now."

"I'm already working for Mrs. Kerner," Sam said. "Just not for money."

"Maybe we have another neighbor who needs help with something," Annabelle said. "Everybody needs help from time to time."

Sam went back to his room and sat on his bed. Who did he know who needed help?

He bet some of his neighbors needed help walking their dogs, and Sam liked dogs a lot. But all the dogs he knew on his street were bigger than he was. Ferguson, the Landrums' bullmastiff, weighed over a hundred pounds. Sam imagined himself flying in the air as he held tight to the squirrel-chasing Ferguson's leash.

That might not be the right job for him.

Did cats take walks? Maybe his neighbor

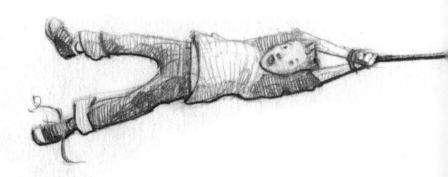

Judy needed someone to walk her cat, Wally. Sam tried to picture a cat on a leash, but he realized he'd never seen one.

But maybe Judy would pay Sam to take her dad, Mr. Stockfish, on a walk! Even very old people like Mr. Stockfish needed exercise, didn't they? And Judy might like to get her dad out of the house, so she could take a turn sitting in his puffy armchair and turning the knob to make it go up and down.

Sam knocked on Judy's door. When she opened it, Sam could hear the all-day news

channel in the next room. The newscaster was reporting on a story about a new polar bear at the zoo.

"Who's at the door?" Mr. Stockfish called to Judy. "Did my package get here?"

"It's Sam from across the street," Judy called back.

"Oh," Mr. Stockfish said. He sounded disappointed.

"Can I get you a glass of lemonade, Sam?" Judy asked.

Sam nodded and then followed Judy to the kitchen.

"Mr. Stockfish watches a lot of TV," he said, sitting down at the kitchen table. "Maybe he should take more walks."

"Yes, he should," Judy agreed. "Only whenever I ask him to take a walk, he refuses. He says walks make his knees hurt. But his doctor says walking would make his knees feel better."

"Maybe I could get him to take a walk," Sam said.

"I wish you'd try," Judy said. "That would be really nice of you."

Sam realized he had made a mistake. Judy thought he was offering to do her a favor. She didn't realize he was asking for a job. Now, if he asked her to pay him, she might get mad.

"Okay," Sam said. He guessed he was stuck with taking Mr. Stockfish on a walk for free.

"In fact," Judy said, handing Sam a glass of lemonade, "I'd pay you to get my dad out of the house. I could use a little 'me time' now and then. How does two dollars a walk sound?"

Sam did the math. Two bucks a pop wasn't twenty bucks a pop, but if he took Mr. Stockfish on ten walks, he'd make twenty bucks in no time and could pay back his dad. So, really, two dollars a walk sounded great.

"I'll take your dad on a walk every day," he said.

"The only problem is you'll have to convince him to get out of that chair."

"Not a problem at all," Sam said. His voice sounded sure, but he didn't feel sure. He had never seen Mr. Stockfish out of his chair. Sam wondered if he slept there. Maybe he never got up!

Then Sam remembered that everyone has to get up to go to the bathroom, even if their knees hurt.

Outside was just a little farther away

than the bathroom. If Mr. Stockfish had to
walk to the bathroom sometimes, then Sam
could get him to walk outside.

At least that was the plan.

Chapter 12

No Talking

Sam had learned an interesting thing about blue eggs.

Everybody wanted to see one.

When Sam got on the bus Monday morning, Miss Louise asked, "Has Helga laid a blue egg yet?"

When he walked into Mr. Pell's classroom, all the kids yelled, "Do you have any blue eggs yet, Sam?"

Every night at dinner his mom said, "I

guess you would have told us if Helga had laid a blue egg today."

Even cranky Mr. Stockfish wanted to see a blue egg.

Sam tried all sorts of ways to make Mr. Stockfish take a walk. He told him walking was the best form of exercise ever. He told him walking would add years to his life. If you had aching joints, taking a walk was a great thing you could do to make them feel better.

Mr. Stockfish wasn't interested. "Walking's boring. I'd rather sit in my chair and watch the news."

Finally, just when he was about to give up, Sam had a brainstorm. "We could walk over to Mrs. Kerner's house and see my chicken, Helga. She lays blue eggs."

That got Mr. Stockfish's attention. "I

had a girlfriend named Helga once," he told Sam. "And her favorite color was blue."

"Then you should come see my chicken," Sam said. "She hasn't actually laid any eggs yet, but she's going to any day. You could be the first person in our neighborhood to see one of Helga's blue eggs."

Mr. Stockfish raised an eyebrow. "I bet a lot of people would like to see that egg first."

"Everybody is very excited about it," Sam said. "The other chickens who live on our street only lay white and brown eggs."

"How many chickens are there on our street?" Mr. Stockfish asked.

"Six besides Helga," Sam said. "They're nice, but their eggs are boring."

Mr. Stockfish reached down and twisted the knob on his chair. Very slowly the back of the chair inched its way up. "Judy!" Mr.

Stockfish yelled. "I need my hat! I'm going to visit a chicken."

That had been on Monday. On Thursday, Sam and Mr. Stockfish were going for their fourth walk, which meant Mr. Stockfish's fourth visit with Helga. Mr. Stockfish, it turned out, liked chickens much better than he liked people.

"Chickens are useful," Mr. Stockfish said as they crossed the street. "People? Not so much."

"Judy's useful," Sam pointed out. "She takes care of you."

"Let me tell you a secret, Sam," Mr. Stockfish said. He leaned down like he was going to whisper in Sam's ear. "I'm the one who takes care of Judy. Sure, she cooks and cleans and does the laundry. But I provide the commentary."

Sam had no idea what Mr. Stockfish was talking about, but he nodded anyway.

When they reached Mrs. Kerner's yard, Sam grabbed two lawn chairs from Mrs. Kerner's deck, so he and Mr. Stockfish could sit by Helga's crate.

"When are you going to put her in the coop with the other chickens?" Mr. Stockfish asked as they sat down. "I bet she's ready."

"As soon she starts laying eggs," Sam said. "I'm afraid if we put her in before she lays an egg, it will take her weeks to calm down."

After that, Sam and Mr. Stockfish didn't say a lot.

Sam was getting used to the fact that Mr. Stockfish didn't like to talk. At first, he thought Mr. Stockfish was going to be like his grandfather—Pop—who took a while to warm up. But once Pop got going, he was hard to stop, especially if he was talking about his favorite topic, tropical fish.

But Mr. Stockfish didn't have a favorite topic. Mostly he just liked watching the chickens. Sam did too, so he didn't mind being quiet. He'd rather listen to Helga cluck. She clucked a lot when she was digging in the dirt for bugs.

Today she was clucking more than usual. Maybe she had found a worm, Sam thought. The most excited he had ever seen Helga was on Tuesday, when she pulled a worm out of the dirt. Sam thought the stretched-out worm looked gross, but Mr. Stockfish clapped his hands and yelled, "Eat him up, Helga!"

"There she goes," Mr. Stockfish said now. Sam turned around. He had been watching the coop, where Queen Bee, the top chicken,

seemed to be arguing with Pretty Girl, the second-chicken-in-command, about whose turn it was at the water dish.

"Look," Mr. Stockfish said. "She's heading for her box."

Helga's box was filled with straw. The open side faced out, so it was like a little house with the front part missing. Helga climbed in and began rocking back and forth.

Sam had seen Helga walk into her box, but she had always walked right back out.

This time it looked like she planned to stay.

Sam and Mr. Stockfish looked at each other. Mr. Stockfish put a finger to his lips. Sam nodded.

Now was definitely not the time for talking.

CHAPTER 13

Sam the Man and the
Blue Egg of Happiness

A few minutes later Helga stood up, shook out her feathers, and exited the nesting box. Sam looked at Mr. Stockfish. Mr. Stockfish looked at Sam.

"Should we check?" Sam asked.

"Crawl on in there!" Mr. Stockfish said. "Take a look!"

"But what if Helga pecks me?"

Mr. Stockfish thought. "I don't think she

will, but you could take her out, just in case. She can sit with me."

"Okay," Sam said. "But I should warn you. She likes to hop."

"I know how to control a chicken," Mr. Stockfish said.

Helga seemed happy to sit in Mr. Stockfish's lap. Mr. Stockfish seemed happy to be holding a chicken. Sam was excited to crawl into Helga's crate. He was nervous, too. Maybe Helga hadn't laid an egg after all. Or if she had, maybe it wouldn't be a blue egg. Or maybe Sam would drop it.

"Quit stalling, Sam!" Mr. Stockfish said. "I want to see an egg, pronto!"

Sam got down on his hands and knees and crawled into the crate. The ground was covered with straw, and the dirt under the straw was a little bit wet. He could feel the knees of his jeans getting a little bit wet too. He tried not to think about the fact that Helga pooped in her crate and that right now he was probably crawling across chicken poop. On the other hand, who cared about chicken poop? Sam was sure it washed right out.

Sam liked being inside Helga's crate. It was cozy. Maybe he could spend the night here sometime.

But first things first. Carefully reaching into the nesting box, Sam felt around in the straw. His fingers touched something hard and smooth. He knew that feeling.

It was the feeling of an egg.

Carefully, Sam picked the egg up and pulled his hand out of the box.

He was holding an egg.

A blue egg!

Sam couldn't believe it! He had waited and waited for Helga to lay an egg, and now she finally had. She was the best chicken ever!

He turned around and proudly showed Helga's egg to Mr. Stockfish. "Ta-da! One blue egg, fresh from the nest! And it's warm!"

"Good girl," Mr. Stockfish told Helga, patting her wing.

Sam scooched backward out of the crate, cradling Helga's blue egg in his right hand, careful not to break it. When he got back to his chair, he showed it to Helga, but she didn't seem interested. Sam was happy. Now, he wouldn't feel guilty about taking Helga's egg away from her.

He and Mr. Stockfish admired the egg. It was light blue and the size of a small

avocado. Everything about it was perfect. It was perfectly smooth and perfectly oval. Sam sniffed it and thought it had a perfect nonsmell.

"Do you have a way to carry it home?" Mr. Stockfish asked.

Sam did not. He'd forgotten to think about that. He couldn't put the egg in his pocket, and he was afraid if he carried it home in his hand, he would drop it.

There was only one solution. Sam untied his shoe and pulled off his sock.

"How about this?" he asked Mr. Stock-fish.

"Does it stink?"

Sam sniffed his sock. "I don't think so. It mostly smells like my shoe, and my shoe doesn't stink. It smells like shoe, too."

"Then I think putting Helga's egg in

90

your sock is a good idea," Mr. Stockfish said. "Just don't forget it's in there and put your sock back on your foot."

"I won't," Sam promised.

Sam put Helga back into her crate, and he and Mr. Stockfish walked back to Judy's house. Sam was so excited about Helga's blue egg, he could feel himself wanting to go fast.

He was glad Mr. Stockfish was there to slow him down.

When Judy opened the door to let Mr. Stockfish in, she was delighted to see the blue egg. "Would you like me to scramble it for you, Sam?"

Sam backed away from the door. "No thank you."

Judy smiled. "I was just kidding. I know you want to show everyone. Don't forget to take a picture, so you'll always remember Helga's first egg."

That was a great idea. Now, Sam had to try extra hard not to run home.

"Annabelle!" he yelled as soon as he got inside his house. "I need to borrow your phone!"

Sam took seventeen pictures of Helga's egg with Annabelle's phone.

He took a picture of his mom holding the egg and a picture of Annabelle holding the egg. Then he put the egg on a pillow on the couch and took eight pictures of it.

"Do you want me to take a picture of you holding Helga's egg?" Annabelle asked, and Sam nodded. He thought that was a good idea. He cradled the egg in his hands and stood very still. Annabelle snapped three pictures.

"You should print one of these out and take it to Helga tomorrow," Annabelle said when she was done taking Sam and the egg's picture. "You could hang it up in her crate."

Sam thought that was a good idea too.

Now, all he had to do was figure out how he was going to carry the egg to school tomorrow without breaking it. He needed something better than his sock. He needed something soft and cushiony. Something that made it 100 percent certain Helga's egg wouldn't break.

Sam knew just the exact right thing.

CHAPTER 14

The Most Famous Egg in the World

The next morning Sam's mom walked out of the downstairs bathroom. "Who used up all the toilet paper?" she asked. "I just put a new roll in yesterday."

"I needed some for my egg," Sam told her. He was eating his breakfast. A few tiny waffle crumbs sprayed from his mouth as he spoke.

"Gross, Sam," Annabelle said, peering over the sports page. "Clean it up."

Sam opened the lid of his box, which was on the table next to his place mat. He tore off a sheet of toilet paper and wiped up his waffle crumbs.

"So that's where it all went to," his mom said. "You made a toilet paper nest."

Sam nodded. "I have to keep Helga's egg safe. It's a pretty bumpy ride to school."

"And you really needed to use the whole roll?"

Sam nodded again. Did his mom really need to ask?

"What's in the box?" Miss Louise asked when Sam got on the bus.

"Helga laid an egg," Sam announced.

"A blue egg?" Miss Louise asked. When Sam nodded, Miss Louise said, "May I see?"

Sam carefully unlatched the box and

opened the lid. As soon as he did, every kid on the bus yelled, "Let me see!"

Miss Louise held up her hand. "Everybody, back in your seats! When we get to school, Sam will let each and every one of you take a look as you step off the bus."

Then she oohed and aahed at Helga's egg. "What a beauty!"

Sam thought so too.

When they got to school, Sam showed all the kids on his bus Helga's blue egg. Miss Louise stood beside him and said, "Don't touch!" every time somebody started to reach out their hand.

Sam thought it was nice that Helga's egg had a bodyguard.

"We will spend five minutes talking about Helga's blue egg," Mr. Pell told Sam's class

after the bell rang. "Then we will get back to our regular schedule."

The class gathered around Sam's box. He told them the story of watching Helga lay her egg. Caitlin Mills asked if Sam had actually seen the blue egg come out of Helga's bottom.

The class seemed very disappointed when Sam said he hadn't.

"Is she going to lay another egg today?" Hutch Mooney asked.

Sam hadn't thought about that. "I guess so. I think most chickens lay an egg every day, as long as they get enough light."

"Are you going to bring an egg to school every day?" Hutch asked. "Or are you going to eat them all for breakfast?"

"I guess we'll eat them," Sam said.

"Can I have the shell?" Margaret Lopez asked. "I'll give you fifty cents."

"Even if it's broken and crunched up?" Sam asked.

"Oh. Maybe not," Margaret said.

"Did you know you don't have to break the shell to get the egg out?" Mr. Pell said. "There's another way to do it."

"Could we do it now?" Hutch asked. "I want to see if the yolk is blue."

"I don't think it is," Sam said. "I think the yolk is regular."

He turned to Mr. Pell. "Can you show me how to get the egg out without cracking the shell?"

Mr. Pell nodded. He went to his desk and got out a small plastic box. "This is my sewing kit," he told the class. "In case a button pops off my shirt during school."

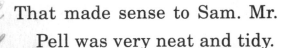

That made sense to Sam. Mr. Pell was very neat and tidy. Taking a needle from his sewing kit, Mr. Pell said, "I'm going to poke two holes in Helga's egg, one on the top and one on the bottom. Then I'm going to blow into the hole on the top. The egg white and yolk will come out of the bottom."

Sam almost couldn't watch. But he needed to, to see how it was done.

Because Sam the Man had a new plan.

He would give the insides of Helga's blue eggs to his mom, who liked to eat eggs for breakfast.

But he would sell the blue shells for fifty cents apiece.

He'd make a fortune.

Mr. Pell's cheeks puffed out and then went back to normal. Puffed out. Normal. Puffed out. Normal.

And then *whoosh!* The egg white and yolk popped out of the hole at the bottom end of the shell and plopped into the coffee cup Mr. Pell had set out to catch them.

Everyone in the class cheered. Mr. Pell handed Sam the eggshell.

"Be careful with it," Mr. Pell said. "It will break even more easily now."

"Can I buy it?" Margaret asked.

"You can buy the next one," Sam told her. "I'm keeping this one."

"In your box?"

Sam nodded. "In my box."

Sam carefully laid the empty eggshell on its nest of toilet paper and closed the lid. Then he latched the latch.

"Can you put this somewhere protected?" he asked Mr. Pell.

Mr. Pell took his lunch bag out of the big bottom drawer of his desk and put the box in. He locked the lock.

"It will be fine in there," he told Sam.

Sam breathed in a deep breath. He let it out.

Finally, he could relax.

The blue egg was safe.

CHAPTER 15

Sam the Man and the Mr. Stockfish Plan

S am Graham didn't need a job anymore.

He had a list of forty-two kids who wanted one of Helga's blue eggshells. Annabelle said she had at least twenty friends who would want one.

Sam Graham was going to be rich.

Very rich.

He spent all of Friday afternoon and Saturday practicing poking holes into eggs and blowing out the whites and yolks.

It took a while to get good at it. He would have gotten better faster, but every five minutes his mom came into the kitchen to complain about the eggs he was using.

"I'll pay you back," Sam promised. "You'll get the insides of all of Helga's eggs."

"I'm keeping track," his mom said. "So far you owe me seven."

It was on egg number nine that Sam finally got the hang of it.

It was on egg number eleven when he remembered he needed to go clean the chicken coop and see if Helga had laid another egg.

When he got to Mrs. Kerner's backyard, Mr. Stockfish was sitting in a lawn chair next to Helga's crate.

Sam had forgotten about taking Mr. Stockfish on his walk.

He'd forgotten the day before, too.

"I think our girl is ready to go in the big coop," Mr. Stockfish said when he saw Sam. "I've been watching her all afternoon. She spends a lot of time looking at the other chickens and clucking. That's a sign."

"Did you walk here by yourself?"

Mr. Stockfish shrugged. "I know the way. I almost tripped, but I grabbed a bush. It was fine."

Sam felt bad. He hadn't meant to quit his job taking Mr. Stockfish out on walks.

"I'll walk you home," he said. "It's not good to trip."

"I didn't trip, though," Mr. Stockfish said. "My knees are getting stronger."

"That's good," Sam said. "Maybe we

could take a longer walk tomorrow. We could walk to the park."

"I like walking here," Mr. Stockfish said. "Here, I am among friends."

"With the chickens?"

"Yes," Mr. Stockfish said. "And you, too, when you don't talk too much."

Sam almost said something, but he didn't.

Instead, he opened the door to Helga's crate. "Would you like to go into the coop today?" he asked her.

"Look at that!" Mr. Stockfish said. "She's nodding!"

Helga walked over to Sam and hopped into his arms. She clucked and squawked and shook out her feathers.

"I guess that means she's ready," Sam said.

"I told you she was ready!" Mr. Stockfish said.

Sam walked over to the coop, holding Helga under his left arm. He opened the coop's door with his right hand. All the chickens came rushing over.

"Don't let them out!" Mr. Stockfish said.

"I won't," Sam told him. He'd been watching the chickens for a while now, and he knew how their minds worked. In fact, he was sort of a chicken expert at this point. He was probably the biggest chicken expert he knew.

He used to only know three things about chickens, but now he knew lots. He knew chickens ate bugs and worms and that they shed their feathers once a year. He knew chickens had a pecking order, and it was important to get along with the head chicken. He knew that their eggs could be different colors. Why, Sam must know a million chicken facts now.

Sam's chest puffed out a little from pride, just like a chicken's.

Standing in front of the coop door, he blocked the chickens with his foot. Then he leaned down and pushed Helga inside.

"Good luck," he told her. "I'll be right here if you need me."

Helga took a step into the coop, and Sam closed the door behind her. Queen Bee walked over and clucked. Helga took a step back.

"Don't let her boss you around, Helga!" Mr. Stockfish said.

Helga took a step forward. Then she took a step sideways. Pretty Girl came over and said hello. At least it seemed to Sam like she was saying hello. He didn't speak chicken, so he didn't know for sure.

Sam stood right outside the coop for five minutes. He wanted to make sure no one was going to peck Helga. No one did. She'd been their neighbor for more than a week now. Sam guessed they were used to her.

Sam sat down in the lawn chair next to Mr. Stockfish. "A bunch of kids are going to buy Helga's eggshells for fifty cents," he said. "I'm going to make a lot of money."

"I see," Mr. Stockfish said. "Then I guess you won't need a job taking me on walks anymore."

Sam guessed he wouldn't. Still, he felt bad. He didn't mind walking with Mr. Stockfish. Sure, they went really slow, but going slow was okay. You noticed more things if you were going slow and not talking.

And just because he didn't need a job, it

didn't mean he couldn't have a job.

But what would he do with the extra money?

Sam looked at Mr. Stockfish looking at the chickens. Mr. Stockfish was nodding and smiling. He enjoyed the chickens very much. Sam enjoyed Mr. Stockfish very much. He was cranky, but he talked to Sam like he was another grown-up, only shorter. And who else besides Mr. Stockfish cared about Helga and Pretty Girl and Queen Bee as much as Sam did?

Just like that, Sam the Man had a plan.

"I would still like to keep my job taking you on walks," he told Mr. Stockfish. "If that's okay with you."

Mr. Stockfish didn't say anything. Then he nodded. "That would be okay with me."

At two dollars a walk he would make

plenty of money in no time. After he paid back his dad, he could call Trish Hardy and see if she had any chickens left.

Sam was going to get a chicken for Mr. Stockfish to put in with Helga and Mrs. Kerner's flock.

Why not? A chicken didn't cost all that much. Twenty bucks a pop.

Worth every penny, Sam thought.

Acknowledgments

All kinds of people have helped Sam make his plans: the very wonderful Caitlyn M. Dlouhy, the equally grand Jessica Sit, and the wise and remarkable Justin Chanda. Thanks go to Sonia Chaghatzbanian, who has made so many of my books look their best, and to Amy June Bates for bringing Sam & Company to life with her illustrations. Thank you, copyeditor Clare McGlade, for doing one of the hardest jobs in publishing. I hope you know you're appreciated.

Thanks, as always, to my friends and family. Thanks especially to Jeff Burch for his support and encouragement. Finally, thanks to Clifton, Jack, and Will Dowell, and to Travis, a very good dog indeed.

What will Sam plan next?
Find out in this sneak peek of
SAM THE MAN & the Rutabaga Plan!

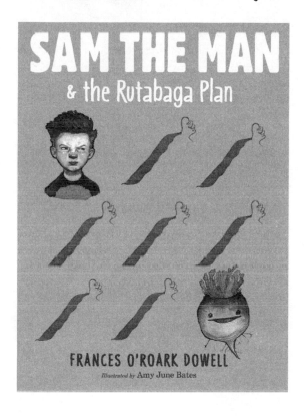

SAM THE MAN
& the Rutabaga Plan

FRANCES O'ROARK DOWELL
Illustrated by Amy June Bates

Welcome to Your Vegetable

Sam Graham was not a vegetable man.

"Two cups a day, Sam," his mom liked to say. "That's all it takes to be healthy."

"That's two cups of important vitamins and minerals, Sam the Man," his dad always added.

"It's two cups of stuff that probably still has dirt on it even though Mom washed it," his sister, Annabelle, usually pointed out.

"I'll eat extra grapes," Sam told his mom whenever she tried to make him eat steamed broccoli or spinach salad. "And three bananas a day."

"Fruit is good," his mom would say. "But you need vegetables, too."

Vegetables, in Sam's opinion, were overrated. They were either too crunchy or too slimy. Most of them looked weird. Especially broccoli. Sam thought broccoli looked unnatural, like it was trying to be a tree but had forgotten to read the instruction manual.

He didn't even want to think about asparagus. You could have nightmares about asparagus.

So when his second-grade teacher, Mr. Pell, announced they were going to start a new science unit first thing Monday morning, and that that unit would be all about vegetables, Sam was glad he had an appointment to get his teeth cleaned.

That was another thing about broccoli—it got stuck in your teeth, and you wouldn't even know it until you looked in the mirror. Sam bet his dentist, Dr. Jenny, hated broccoli as much as he did.

"Actually, Sam, broccoli is a good source of calcium, and calcium is good for your teeth and bones," Dr. Jenny told him that Monday morning. She was poking at his gums with a dental pick. "If you floss after you eat, you don't have to worry about broccoli in your teeth, now do you?"

Sam guessed not. "But what if I forget to floss?" he asked. "Because sometimes I do, and then there's all that broccoli stuck in there. It's gross."

Dr. Jenny raised her eyebrow. "Do you floss every day?"

"Most of the time," Sam said.

"Almost all of the time?" Dr. Jenny asked.

"Almost most of some of the time," Sam said.

Sam left Dr. Jenny's office with four trial-sized packs of dental floss and a booklet called *Flossing: How to Be Your Teeth's Best Friend!*

Sam didn't know his teeth even had friends.

"The point is, you need to floss," his mom said as she signed him in at the front office when they got to school. "Your plaque score was a five!"

"But no cavities!" Sam said. He smiled as big as he could, so his mom could see all his perfect teeth.

Walking down the hall to his class-room, Sam felt happy that he had missed science, even if his plaque score was five. He would rather have plaque than learn about vegetables any day.

"Good morning, Sam!" Mr. Pell greeted him when Sam walked into Room 11. "I hope you're ready to learn about the wonderful world of vegetables. For the next two weeks, you and a very special vegetable are going to get to know each other. You're going to study your vege-table, write about your vegetable, and teach us a thing or two about your vege-table."

"What do you mean, *my* vegetable?" Sam asked.

The other kids started to giggle. That's

when Sam noticed that everyone had a vegetable on his or her desk.

Gavin had a carrot.

Will had a head of cabbage.

Rashid had a tiny pumpkin.

Emily had a green bean.

Marja had an eggplant.

There was something on Sam's desk too, only he didn't know what it was.

It was the size of a softball.

It was round, but not perfectly round.

One half was purple, and the other half was a dirty yellow.

There was a weird brown thing sticking out of the top like a little tree stump.

"What is *that*?" Sam asked.

"It's a rutabaga!" Will yelled. Everybody started laughing, and Gavin laughed so hard he fell out of his seat.

Mr. Pell came over to Sam's desk. "Sam," he said, "I'd like to introduce you to your vegetable. I think the two of you are about to become very good friends."

Sam Graham the Rutabaga Man

Sam was now sorry he'd had his teeth cleaned.

In first period, while Dr. Jenny was poking at Sam's gums, everyone else was choosing a vegetable. They had all pulled numbers from a paper bag, and the person who picked 1 (Emily) got to choose first, and the person who picked 2 (Hutch) got to choose second, and so on.

Because Sam hadn't been there, he got

last pick, which is how he got stuck with a rutabaga for the next two weeks. And now for homework he had to write a one-page letter from his rutabaga's point of view.

Sam was pretty sure vegetables didn't have a point of view.

But even if some vegetables *did* have a point of view, like maybe carrots or peas, he was positive that rutabagas didn't. A carrot might say, *My favorite color is orange*, and that would make sense. *It scares me when I roll under the table*, a pea might tell you, and you'd understand.

But a rutabaga? What would a rutabaga have to say about anything?

"It probably has a lot of opinions about dirt," Sam's neighbor Mr. Stockfish said after school that day. Mr. Stockfish and Sam were feeding chickens in the coop behind Mrs. Kerner's house. Sam had two after-school jobs: walking Mr. Stockfish and taking care of chickens. He was responsible for eight chickens in all, including his own chicken, Helga, who laid blue eggs, and Mr. Stockfish's chicken, Leroy, who laid regular white eggs.

Sam poured two cups of grain into the chickens' feeder. "Why would a rutabaga have an opinion on dirt?" he asked.

"Because it's a root vegetable," Mr. Stockfish said. "It does all its growing underground."

"So, it lives in the dark until somebody eats it? That's its whole life?"

"What's so bad about that?" Mr. Stockfish asked. He was sitting in a lawn chair. He called himself the chicken

supervisor, which meant Sam did the work while Mr. Stockfish watched.

"It's boring! And you're surrounded by dirt all the time!"

"What are they teaching at that school of yours?" Mr. Stockfish asked. "Dirt is one of the most interesting things in the world. Did you know there are more than ten thousand different kinds of bacteria in one teaspoon of soil?"

"That makes dirt sound very unhealthy," Sam said.

Mr. Stockfish snorted and shook his head.

"There's a lot you don't know about bacteria, Sam," he said. "Bacteria makes the world go 'round."

"Well, I wish bacteria was a vegetable, then," Sam said. "It sounds like it would be a much better project than a rutabaga."

After Sam gave the chickens their water, he plopped in the lawn chair next to Mr. Stockfish. He wondered if chickens ate rutabagas. Maybe that's what his rutabaga's letter could be about. *Dear Mom, Today I got eaten by eight chickens. Now I'm dead. Bye.*

Sam liked that idea. If his rutabaga got eaten by chickens, then Mr. Pell would have to give him another vegetable. Maybe he'd get a banana pepper next time. Sam could think of lots of things a banana pepper might write a letter about. *Dear Mom, Today I took a ride in a pizza box to a boy named Sam's house. . . .*

"Chickens don't eat rutabagas," Mr. Stockfish said when Sam told him his plan. "What are you, crazy?"

Sam decided to look it up when he got home. But first he would have to get his mom's permission to use her computer.

"I'm working," his mom said when he knocked on her office door. Sam's mom worked at home some days and at an office across town the other days. When she worked at home, Sam was only supposed to knock on her door if he had an emergency situation.

Sam was pretty sure having to do a

rutabaga project counted as an emergency situation.

"You want to feed your rutabaga to the chickens so you can do another vegetable?" his mom said when Sam explained why he needed to go on the Internet. "Do you think that's fair?"

"To the rutabaga or the chickens?" Sam asked.

"I mean, to, well, the other kids, I guess," his mom said. She sounded like she wasn't sure what she meant. "What if everyone fed their vegetables to chickens in order to get a new one?"

"But I'm the only person in my class with a chicken," Sam said. "A lot of people have dogs, but I don't think dogs like vegetables."

His mother sighed. "Sorry, Sam. You're

stuck with your rutabaga. If the chickens ate the one you have now, we'd just go to the store and buy another one. So you better get started on your letter."

Sam went to his room, sat down at his desk, and opened his science notebook. He picked up his pencil. He put his pencil down. He picked it up again and chewed on the end, and then he wondered if he had yellow pencil bits in his teeth.

Maybe I should floss, Sam thought. Yes, he should floss. He put his pencil down.

The rutabaga letter would have to wait.